BIRDBRAIN AMOS

MR. FUN

MICHAEL DELANEY

PHILOMEL BOOKS

THIS WAY TO THE
SERENGETI

For Emma and the cousins . . .
Esa, Eily, Grace, Phoebe, Greg, Kate, Callie, Becky,
Archie, Mackie, Jamie, Nicholas and Alex.

PHILOMEL BOOKS A division of Penguin Young Readers Group. Published by The Penguin Group. Penguin Group (USA) Inc., 375 Hudson Street, New York, NY 10014, U.S.A. Penguin Group (Canada), 90 Eglinton Avenue East, Suite 700, Toronto, Ontario, Canada M4P 2Y3 (a division of Pearson Penguin Canada Inc.). Penguin Books Ltd, 80 Strand, London WC2R 0RL, England. Penguin Ireland, 25 St. Stephen's Green, Dublin 2, Ireland (a division of Penguin Books Ltd.). Penguin Group (Australia), 250 Camberwell Road, Camberwell, Victoria 3124, Australia (a division of Pearson Australia Group Pty Ltd). Penguin Books India Pvt Ltd, 11 Community Centre, Panchsheel Park, New Delhi - 110 017, India. Penguin Group (NZ), Cnr Airborne and Rosedale Roads, Albany, Auckland 1310, New Zealand (a division of Pearson New Zealand Ltd). Penguin Books (South Africa) (Pty) Ltd, 24 Sturdee Avenue, Rosebank, Johannesburg 2196, South Africa.

Penguin Books Ltd, Registered Offices: 80 Strand, London WC2R 0RL, England.

 Published simultaneously in Canada. Printed in the United States of America. Design by Gina DiMassi. The illustrations are rendered in pen and ink on watercolor paper. Library of Congress Cataloging-in-Publication Data   Delaney, M. C. (Michael Clark)   Birdbrain Amos, Mr. Fun / Michael Delaney.   p. cm.   Summary: Amos the hippopotamus takes his tick bird, Amoeba, and her family on what he hopes will be a fun vacation, but he finds himself competing with Amoeba's imaginary friend. [1. Hippopotamus—Fiction. 2. Cattle egret—Fiction. 3. Friendship—Fiction. 4. Imaginary playmates—Fiction. 5. Africa—Fiction.] I. Title.   PZ7.D37319Bio 2006   [Fic]—dc22   2005023844   ISBN 0-399-24278-3

1 3 5 7 9 10 8 6 4 2

First Impression

Chapter One
NOTHING TO DO

In many respects, Amos was like any other hippopotamus you might stumble upon in the jungles of Africa. He was big and gray and lived along a wide, lazy-flowing river that was surrounded by the juiciest green vegetation. Like any other hippopotamus, Amos loved to hang out in the water, especially on hot, steamy days. Because he lived in one of the most tropical places on Earth, that was pretty much nearly all the time.

There was one way, though, in which Amos was not like any other hippopotamus. He had a bird's nest on top of his head. It was a small bird's nest, about the size of a cereal bowl, but it was a bird's nest, just the same.

It wasn't Amos's idea to keep a bird's nest on top of his head. It belonged to a little tick bird named Amoeba (a-mee-ba). Her mother, Kumba, had built the nest. It was made of grass, feathers, reeds, and mud. It sat upon Amos's immense bald head, right between his ears.

One broiling hot afternoon Amos was doing what he always did on a broiling hot afternoon: He was lying in the muddy river, just loafing around. Suddenly, from on top of his head, Amos heard a forlorn little sigh. Then he heard a forlorn little voice say, "There's nothing to do!"

Amos peered at his reflection in the river. He could see Amoeba's reflection, too. The little bird was slumped in her nest, looking very bored.

"What do you mean there's nothing to do?" he asked. "There are lots of things to do."

"Like what?" asked Amoeba.

"Well, for one thing, you can get rid of some bugs," said Amos. "I think I feel one crawling up my back."

"I'm tired of getting wid of bugs!" replied Amoeba. (Amoeba, who was not quite a year old yet, had trouble pronouncing certain words, particularly certain words with the letter "r" in them.)

"Well, then, take a nap," suggested Amos. "That's what I do when I have nothing to do."

"That's no fun!" replied Amoeba. "I want to do something fun! We never do anything fun!"

"What do you mean?" asked Amos. "We do lots of fun things!"

"Like what?"

"Well, like . . ."

Amos paused, trying to think of something.

"*See?*" cried Amoeba. "You can't think of anything!"

"I can think of something," said Amos. "I just can't think of something right this minute."

"Well, while you're trying to think of something, I'm going to go find something fun to do!" said Amoeba.

And before Amos could say another word, Amoeba flew off across the river.

Chapter Two
ZAMU'S IDEA OF FUN

Amos sighed. He did not like to see his friend so unhappy. He did not like to hear his friend say the two of them never did anything fun together. What was Amoeba talking about? They did lots of fun things together.

Didn't they?

Amos decided he needed to find some fun things to do with Amoeba. The only problem was, he couldn't think of anything fun to do right at that moment. So he decided to get someone else's idea on the subject.

"I'll ask my friend Zamu," he said.

Amos found Zamu just down the river. The huge hippopotamus was sprawled out on the muddy riverbank with his eyes closed, basking in the bright sun.

"Excuse me, Zamu," said Amos as he emerged, dripping wet, from the river. "I have a question for you. What's your idea of fun?"

"I'm doing it," replied Zamu in a sleepy voice, without even opening his eyes.

"Well, if you were going to do something else," said Amos, "what would you do?"

Zamu opened one eye. "Why do you ask?"

"I'm just wondering," said Amos.

Zamu opened his other eye and sat up. "You're not planning on getting me a bird's nest, are you?"

"A bird's nest?" said Amos.

"Yes, a bird's nest," said Zamu. He scowled at the bird's nest on top of Amos's head. "Because if you are, Amos, that's *not* my idea of fun."

"It isn't?" said Amos.

"No, it isn't!" cried Zamu. "Don't even think of getting me a bird's nest, Amos! I won't wear it!"

"Don't worry, Zamu," said Amos. "I won't get you a bird's nest."

"You better not!" replied Zamu. "Because if you think that's *my* idea of fun, Amos, you're a bigger birdbrain than I thought!"

Chapter Three
THE RIDDLE

Amos decided to get someone else's idea of fun. Someone who wasn't quite so grumpy. He spotted Kumba, Amoeba's mother, farther up the shore, flitting about among the tall reeds.

"What luck!" thought Amos. If anyone knew what Amoeba's idea of fun was, it would be her mother!

Amos trotted over. "Hi, Kumba!" he said. "What's your idea of fun?"

Kumba lighted upon a reed. She peered curiously at Amos and said, "Is this a riddle?"

"I don't think so," replied Amos.

"It sounds like a riddle," said Kumba.

"Well, it's not," said Amos.

"Don't you think it sounds like a riddle?" she asked.

"Yes, I suppose it does sound like one," admitted Amos. "But it's not a riddle."

"Maybe it should be a riddle," said Kumba. "Have you ever thought of that?"

"No, I can't say that I have," said Amos.

"If it were a riddle, what do you think the answer would be?"

"I don't know," said Amos.

"It's got to have an answer if it's going to be a riddle," said Kumba.

"Yes, I agree," said Amos. "Now back to my question, Kumba. What is your idea of fun?"

"I didn't realize a tick bird and a hippopotamus could have so much in common," said the hippo.

"Well, we're not any old tick bird and hippopotamus! Are we, Amos?"

"Well, we're not all *that* different from other tick birds and hippopotamuses," said Amos.

Akka, grinning, pointed his wing at Amos. "Will you listen to this guy!" he said. "So, what can I do for you, Amos?"

"I thought that was my question," said Kumba.

"No, I think it was *my* question," said Amos.

"I don't think so, Amos," said Kumba. "I think it was *my* question. If you recall, I said that if it's going to be a riddle, it's got to have an answer. Then I asked you what the answer would be. And now you're asking *me* what the answer would be. So you see, Amos, it's really my question, not yours."

As Kumba was saying this, Amos realized something. He realized that perhaps Kumba was not the best one to ask about fun things to do. He decided he should seek someone else's advice.

"Well, thank you, Kumba, for all your help," he said, and he slipped back into the river.

Chapter Four
TWINS

Amos swam downstream. Over in a lagoon, he spotted a huge hippopotamus lying in the reeds and lily pads. A tick bird was hopping about on the hippo's back, searching for bugs and ticks to eat. Amos did not know the hippopotamus, but he recognized the tick bird the moment he saw him. It was none other than Amoeba's father, Akka.

Amos swam right over. "Akka, you're just the bird I'm looking for!" he cried.

The hippopotamus turned and gazed curiously at Amos. He was Akka's new boss. The hippo had hired Akka to get rid of his bugs and ticks.

"Oh, hello!" said Amos, smiling, to the hippo. "My name is Amos. I'm a friend of Akka's."

Akka flew down to a lily pad. "That's a understatement, Amos!" he said. "You an are more than just friends! We're practic twins!"

"Twins?" said the hippopotamus, op his eyes wide in astonishment.

"That's right!" said Akka. "Amo are just alike! We think alike! We We're just like twins! Right, Amo

"Well, I wouldn't exactly say t Amos.

"See that?" cried Akka, chuc is so modest, he won't even like me!"

"I'm looking for something fun to do," said Amos.

"*Fun?*" asked Akka.

"Yes, fun," said Amos. "I'm hoping you might be able to help me think of something."

"Amos, you've come to the right bird!" said Akka.

This was just what Amos wanted to hear. "So what's your idea of fun?" he asked.

"A vacation!" replied Akka.

"A vacation?" said Amos.

"Yes, a vacation!" said Akka.

The hippo, listening, nodded in agreement. "Akka is right," he said. "But it can't be just any vacation."

"No?" said Amos, peering at the hippo.

The hippo shook his head and said, "No. It's got to be a *fun* vacation!"

"Absolutely!" agreed Akka.

This sounded great to Amos. No, it sounded better than great. It sounded fantastic! There was only one problem. Amos had never been on a vacation before, let alone a *fun* vacation.

"How do I find out how to go on a *fun* vacation?" he asked.

Akka chuckled. "Amos, my friend," he said, "that is what travel agents are for."

Chapter Five
THE TRAVEL AGENT

Amos peered at Akka. "A travel agent?" he said. "What's a travel agent?"

"A travel agent is someone who knows all the places to go on vacation," said Akka.

"All the *fun* places," said the hippo.

"Really?" said Amos. He had no idea such an animal existed. "Where do I find a travel agent?"

"Well, it just so happens," said Akka, "that I met a travel agent in my travels. You'll find her office in a dead tree just up the river."

Amos set off immediately. He had no trouble finding the dead tree. Its top branches, choked with vines, towered high above the other leafy trees against the blue African sky.

Amos stepped ashore. He began to make his way through the thick green vegetation. It was not easy. The jungle was very dense. At one point, Amos got all tangled up in some bushes and droopy vines. Amos lowered his head and pushed with all his might. Suddenly, he broke free. He burst out into a small grassy clearing—right at the trunk of the big dead tree.

A vulture stood in the tall grass, bent over, eating lunch. She looked up at Amos, startled.

"Oh, excuse me!" said Amos. "I didn't mean to barge in on you!"

"Dumph be filly!" said the vulture, with

her beak full of food. "Whumph cumph I domph forph yumph toophay?"

"I beg your pardon?" said Amos. He tried not to glance down at the vulture's feet. He did not want to see what poor creature was lunch.

The vulture, swallowing, said, "Don't be silly! What can I do for you today?"

"Well," said Amos. "I'm looking for a travel agent."

"That would be me!" said the vulture.

"You?" said Amos, surprised.

"Yes, me!" said the vulture. She stretched her long neck out, eyeing Amos closely. "Say, don't I know you?" she asked.

"I don't think so," replied Amos.

"Yes, I do know you!" cried the vulture. "You're the hippo who once interviewed me for a job!"

"I am?" said Amos.

"You were looking for a bird to get rid of all your bugs and ticks," said the vulture. "But did you hire me? *No!*"

"That's because I found another bird," said Amos. "I hope there are no hard feelings."

The vulture smiled. "No hard feelings at all!" she said. "And just to show you, let me give you a big kiss."

Before Amos could say a word, the vulture threw both her wings around Amos's thick neck. She gave him a huge wet smacker on the cheek.

Amos, shuddering, leaped back.

"Mmm! Tasty!" murmured the vulture. Then she said, "As you can see, I've found another job. I'm now a travel agent."

"That's why I'm here," said Amos. "I'm hoping you might be able to help me. I need to find somewhere fun to go on vacation."

The vulture's face lit up. "I know *just* the place!" she cried.

Chapter Six
THE SERENGETI

Amos was perfectly delighted that the vulture knew of a fun place to go on vacation. "Where?" he asked.

"How does a fun-filled trip to the Serengeti sound?" said the vulture.

"The Serengeti?" said Amos.

"Yes, the Serengeti!" said the vulture. "One of Africa's most populated wildlife spots!"

"It sounds great!" exclaimed Amos.

"I thought you might like that idea!" said the vulture, beaming.

"Is it very far away?" asked Amos.

"Just a three-day trip down the river," replied the vulture.

"I'm on my way!" said Amos.

"Wait!" cried the vulture. "That's not all! I know just what you should do once you get there!"

"What?" asked Amos excitedly.

"Go on a meat-tasting tour! You'll love every minute of it. You'll get to taste the most exotic animals. Elephants. Rhinos. Jackals. Hyenas. Wildebeests. Not to mention a wide variety of small mammals and birds of many different species."

"That's a wonderful suggestion," said Amos. "The only thing is, I'm a hippopotamus, and hippopotamuses don't eat meat. We're vegetarians."

"Oh, one of *those*," muttered the vulture

23

in disgust. Then her face brightened. "Well, this vacation will change your mind about eating meat. You'll get to taste giraffes, lions, cheetahs, zebras . . ."

The vulture's eyes twinkled as she rattled off animal after animal.

"Oh, the meat is so tender, so scrumptious, so yummy-yum!" The vulture gazed wistfully at Amos and said, "Not unlike the way *you* must taste!"

The vulture had crept very close to Amos. Uncomfortably close. Amos could feel her warm breath on his wet gray skin. She was so close, Amos began to tremble.

"Well, I should probably get going now," said Amos. "Thank you for all the good advice."

"You have to leave? So soon?" said the vulture. She sounded very disappointed. "Are you sure?"

"Yes, I'm quite sure," said Amos. He spun about and dashed back through the jungle. When he got to the river, Amos did not take his time wading into the water the way he usually did.

He plunged right in.

Chapter Seven
BIG NEWS

Amos swam out into the middle of the river. He was very excited. The Serengeti sounded like a marvelous place for him and Amoeba to go on vacation. Who knew a vulture would have such a good travel tip?

Amos could not wait to tell Amoeba about the vacation he had planned. He could not wait to see the little tick bird's face when he told her about the Serengeti and all the animals they would see and all the fun they were going to have.

"And she thinks I don't know how to have fun," thought Amos, chuckling to himself as he swam back up the river.

Amos spied Amoeba hopping about on an old, mossy log that was lying on the shore. The log was half on land, half in the river.

"There you are!" cried Amos as he swam over to Amoeba. "Have I got big news to tell you!"

"Have I got big news to tell you!" said Amoeba.

"What's your big news?" asked Amos.

"You tell me your big news first," said Amoeba.

"No, you first," said Amos.

"No, you!" said Amoeba.

"All right, I'll go first," said Amos.

"No, I want to go first!" said Amoeba.

"Okay, you go first," said Amos.

"Guess what I found?"

"What?" asked Amos.

"A best fwiend!"

Amos, startled, stared at the little bird. "You found a best friend?"

"Her name is Nungwe!" said Amoeba. "She's a little tick bird—like me!"

"That's . . . that's wonderful news, Amoeba," said Amos. He did not really mean it, though. The truth was, Amos thought it was horrible news. He just assumed *he* was Amoeba's best friend. But evidently, he wasn't. Amos knew he had only himself to blame. "I should've been more fun," he told himself.

"What's your big news?" asked Amoeba.

Amos sighed. His big news did not seem so big anymore. "Well . . . ," he said, "I found something fun we could do together."

"You did?" said Amoeba. "What? Tell me! Tell me!"

"I thought we could go on vacation to the Serengeti," said Amos.

"Wow! The Soowoongetti! That sounds fun!" cried Amoeba excitedly. Then she asked, "What is the Soowoongetti?"

"You mean the Serengeti," said Amos.

"That's what I said!" cried Amoeba.

"It's a place with lots and lots of animals," said Amos.

"That sounds like lots and lots of fun!" cried Amoeba. "Can Nungwe come, too?"

"Nungwe?" said Amos. The thought of taking Amoeba's new best friend, Nungwe, to the Serengeti did not sound like fun to Amos. Oh, sure, it might be fun for Amoeba and Nungwe. But not for Amos.

"Please can Nungwe come, too?" begged Amoeba. "Please! Please! Please!"

"I'm sorry, Amoeba, but I don't think so," said Amos.

Amoeba, pouting, crossed her wings and stamped her foot. Then, turning, she said, "Sorry, Nungwe, but Amos says you can't come!"

Amos glanced about, but he did not see any other bird—or any other creature, for that matter—on the log.

"Nungwe is here?" he asked, bewildered. "Are you sure?"

"Yes, I'm sure!"

Amos looked to see if Nungwe was hiding on the other side of the log. Nope, no bird.

"Where is Nungwe?" he asked.

"Wight here!" replied Amoeba.

"Right where?"

"*Wight here!*" said Amoeba. She pointed her wing to her left side.

But no bird was there.

Chapter Eight

NUNGWE

Amos was very puzzled. How could a tick bird be there but not be there? Then, suddenly, it dawned on Amos who Nungwe was and why he could not see her.

She wasn't real. She was an imaginary friend.

"Oh!" Amos blurted out. He focused his eyes on the spot on the log that Amoeba had pointed to. "Hello there!" he said cheerfully.

Amoeba frowned. "Who are you talking to?"

"Why, Nungwe, of course," said Amos.

"Nungwe isn't there!"

"She isn't?"

Amoeba shook her head. She pointed her wing to the other side of her and said, "Nungwe flew over here."

"Oh!" said Amos. He focused his eyes on that side of Amoeba. "Hello, Nungwe!" he said, smiling.

"Nungwe just flew off!" said Amoeba. "She doesn't want to talk to you!"

Amos stopped smiling. "Why not?" he asked.

"She doesn't like *you*!"

"She doesn't?" said Amos. His feelings were hurt. Then he remembered Nungwe wasn't a real bird. "Why doesn't Nungwe like me?"

"Because you won't let her come with us!" replied Amoeba.

"Is that all?" said Amos, chuckling. "Well, I've changed my mind. Nungwe can come with us."

"She can?"

"Absolutely!" said Amos. Now that Amos knew Nungwe was not a real bird, he didn't mind her coming along. Not at all. "We leave first thing tomorrow morning!"

As Amos was saying this, Kumba, Amoeba's mother, appeared in the sky across the river, flying toward them. She touched down on the log beside Amoeba.

"Guess where we're going?" said Amoeba happily.

"Where?" asked Kumba.

"The Soowoon . . . the Soowoon . . ." Amoeba peered up at Amos for help.

"The Serengeti," said Amos.

"We leave first thing tomowwow morning!" said Amoeba.

Kumba's face lit up. "We do!" she cried, thrilled, her eyes bulging. "Oh, I've *always* wanted to go to the Serengeti!"

"You have?" said Amos. "Well, um, uh, the only thing is, Kumba—well, you see—"

"Wait till Akka hears!" blurted out Kumba. "He'll be delighted to hear we're all going to the Serengeti!"

"Akka?" cried Amos.

"You know who else would just love to go?" said Kumba. "My dear friend Cha!"

"*Cha?*" cried Amos, horrified. He remembered how angry Cha had been with him for ruining Kumba's baby shower.

"Cha is always talking about going to the Serengeti!" cried Kumba. "Oh, wait till she hears we're going! She'll be so excited!" Then, taking a hop, Kumba flew off.

"Kumba, wait!" Amos called out.

But Kumba was so excited and flying so fast, she was already halfway across the river—and out of hearing range.

Amos groaned. Now, in addition to Amoeba, three other tick birds would be on vacation with him—*four* when you counted Nungwe!

Chapter Nine
WE NEED TO TALK

I better go find Nungwe and tell her we're leaving first thing tomowwow morning!" cried Amoeba and then she, too, darted off.

As Amos watched the little bird fly up the river, he was perfectly miserable. His vacation was ruined. Totally ruined! And to think he had not even left for vacation yet! Amos just wanted to flop down on the ground and sulk. But he couldn't. He was leaving for vacation first thing in the morning. There was much to do. One thing Amos had to do was tell his friend Zamu that he would be gone for a few days. He did not want Zamu or any of his other hippopotamus friends to worry about him when they found out he was gone.

Amos was about to go look for Zamu when, down the river, he heard a voice cry out, "Not so fast, Amos!"

Amos turned and saw a large hippopotamus swimming toward him. It was Akka's boss. But Akka was not with him. The hippo was all by himself. He looked very distressed about something.

"You and I need to talk, Amos!" said the hippopotamus.

"We do?" said Amos.

"Yes, we do!" replied the hippo. "Tell me the truth, Amos. Who's more like you, me or Akka?"

"Excuse me?" said Amos.

"Who's got more in common with you? Me or Akka?"

"Well, to be quite honest, I hardly know you," said Amos.

"I've got to have more in common with you than Akka!" cried the hippo. "I mean, he's just a tick bird! I'm a hippopotamus— like you! He eats bugs. Do you eat bugs? I don't eat bugs. He's a bird. He can fly. I can't fly. Can you fly? What's your favorite color? Mine's green. What's your favorite thing to eat? I like tall reeds. How about you?"

"Look, I'm a little busy at the moment," said Amos. "Could we discuss this some other time?"

"Absolutely!" said the hippo. "And don't you worry, Amos. I understand completely. I'm the exact same way when I get busy. You think Akka would be as understanding as me? I don't think so!"

"Well, thank you for being so understanding," said Amos, and he turned to leave.

"Do you know why I'm so understanding?" the hippo called after Amos. "Because I'm just like you. If anyone is your twin, Amos, it's me, not Akka! I'm big like you. I'm gray like you. I've got whiskers like you. I have four hooves like you . . ."

Chapter Ten
LET THE VACATION BEGIN!

As it turned out, Amos had no trouble finding Zamu. In fact, the hippopotamus was right where Amos had left him. He was still lying on the muddy riverbank with his eyes closed, sunning himself.

"You're in my sun!" grumbled Zamu when Amos came up to see him.

"Oh, sorry!" said Amos, and he stepped out of Zamu's sun.

Amos waited for Zamu to open his eyes. But he didn't.

"I'm leaving to go on a vacation to-morrow," said Amos. "I was wondering if you could keep an eye on things while I'm away."

Zamu cracked open an eye and peered up at Amos. "I'm not keeping an eye on that bird's nest," he replied, squinting in the bright sunlight. "So if you're thinking of leaving it behind for me to keep an eye on, *don't!*"

"Don't worry, Zamu, I won't be leaving it behind," said Amos. "This nest goes pretty much wherever I go."

Amos thought Zamu would be interested in hearing about his vacation plans. But apparently, he was not. As Amos watched, the big hippopotamus shut his eyes. Then, with a loud snore, Zamu fell back to sleep. Amos, sighing, trudged into the river.

That night Amos stayed up very late.

Hippos tend to stay up late as a rule, anyway, but that night Amos stayed up much later than usual. He found he could not sleep. He was too upset about having to go on vacation in the morning with Akka, Kumba, and Cha. This wasn't Amos's idea of a fun vacation, that was for sure.

It was nearly dawn when Amos finally dozed off. It seemed as if he had just closed his eyes when he heard a loud, disgruntled female voice say, "I thought you said we were leaving first thing in the morning!"

Amos opened his eyes. There, standing in the tall grass in front of him, were Cha, Akka, Kumba, and Amoeba.

"About time!" muttered Cha.

"Good morning, Amos!" boomed Akka, with a big cheerful smile. "All ready to go on vacation?"

"As ready as I'll ever be," sighed Amos, lumbering to his feet.

The tick birds flew up onto Amos. Amoeba, as usual, plopped down in her nest. Kumba and Cha also sat down on Amos's head. Akka, meanwhile, perched himself at the very end of Amos's big nose.

Once everyone was aboard, Amos waded into the river and let the current carry him off. Akka, facing downriver, lifted his wings up into the air and joyfully cried out, "Let the vacation begin!"

Chapter Eleven

HOMESICK

It was nice and peaceful being on the river at such an early hour. (Amos, who tended to be a late riser, wasn't usually on the river at this time of day.) As Amos floated along, the morning sun fell through the thick leaves that hung above the river. Golden sunlight dappled the greenish-brown water.

Akka made himself comfortable at the end of Amos's nose. He sat back against Amos's left nostril and put the tips of his wings behind his head. This gave Akka a perfect view of Amos's face—and Amos a perfect, if rather cross-eyed, view of Akka.

"Ah!" said Akka. "This is the life, isn't it, Amos?"

"I suppose," mumbled Amos.

"You don't sound very happy, Amos," said Akka, eyeing Amos worriedly. Then he burst into a big grin.

"I know what's troubling you!" he cried. "You're homesick! You're just like me! I, too, used to get horribly homesick whenever I left home. Don't worry, Amos. A couple of hours into the trip and you'll feel lots better."

As Akka was saying this, another conversation was happening on top of Amos's head. Actually, two other conversations. Kumba and Cha were gossiping about Cha's boss, a black rhino. Meanwhile, Amoeba was chattering away to her imaginary friend, Nungwe.

Amos groaned to himself. "Some vacation!" he thought.

By and by, Amos floated around a bend. He let out a startled gasp. Hundreds of crocodiles sat in the water, motionless, clogging up the river.

Amos lurched to a stop to avoid ramming into the crocodiles. He stopped so quickly and so abruptly that poor Akka, lounging on the tip of Amos's nose, was hurled, headfirst, into the river.

"Akka!" cried Kumba.

Akka, splashing about, quickly pulled himself back up onto Amos's nose. "What happened?" he asked.

"Sorry about that, Akka," said Amos as he gazed at all the crocodiles. "Traffic jam."

"What a mess!" muttered Cha.

Chapter Twelve
THE TRAFFIC JAM

For several minutes, Amos sat in the river, paddling in place, waiting for the crocodiles to move. But the crocodiles did not move. The traffic did not budge.

Suddenly, from on top of his head, Amos heard Cha grumble, right into his ear, "So we're just going to sit here all day?"

Amos took this as a hint that he should do something.

"Um, excuse me," Amos said to the crocodile that was stuck in front of him. "Any idea what's causing the delay?"

The crocodile did not turn around. He

merely replied in a gruff voice, "Rush hour traffic! It's like this every morning!"

"Oh, okay," said Amos. "Thank you."

"It's rush hour traffic," Amos explained to his passengers. "It's like this every morn—"

"We heard!" replied Cha.

Amos was perfectly content to sit and wait. But not Cha. Amos could feel Cha growing more and more restless on top of his head.

She sighed.

She tapped her foot.

She muttered to herself.

She paced.

She muttered some more.

Finally, Cha bellowed out, "Come on,

fellas, move it! We don't have all day! Let's get this show on the road!"

The crocodile in front of Amos swung around. He glowered at Amos. Evidently, he thought it was *Amos* who had yelled at him.

"What do you want me to do about it, pal?" he snarled. "Can't you see I'm in the same situation as you?"

The last thing Amos wanted was to cause a big scene. He gave the crocodile a friendly smile. He was hoping the crocodile would relax and turn around. But the crocodile did not relax and turn around. He kept staring at Amos with big wide eyes. He made Amos very uneasy.

"Say," said the crocodile, "that isn't a— no, it can't be!" Then his eyes widened even more. "For crying out loud, it *is*! It's a bird's nest! Yo, crocs, check it out! This hippo has a bird's nest on top of his head!"

"Oh, no!" Amos groaned to himself.

The crocodiles turned and gaped at Amos. A few of them gasped. All of them looked shocked and horrified.

A surprising thing happened then. The crocodiles began to move away from Amos.

"Get away!" cried one crocodile. "He must have something wrong with him!"

The crocodiles pushed and shoved each other to get as far away from Amos as possible. This, in turn, opened up a wide channel for Amos to swim down.

Amos felt a sharp peck on top of his head. "Don't just sit there like a dolt!" barked Cha. "Get moving!"

Amos got moving. Within minutes, he and the tick birds were back in the open water, floating down the river.

"Now *this* is more like it!" declared Cha.

Chapter Thirteen
THE CROCODILE

As Amos swam down the river, he heard a voice call out from behind him, "Hey, buddy, wait!"

Amos turned and saw a crocodile swimming furiously toward him. A somewhat large white bird with somewhat long legs was perched on top of the crocodile's bumpy head.

"Whew!" said the crocodile. "I thought I'd never catch up with you!"

"Can I help you?" asked Amos.

"I see you have a lot of tick birds on you," said the crocodile. "You must have a real bad problem with bugs."

"We're on vacation!" replied Akka.

"You are?" said the crocodile. He swam closer to Amos. As he did, Amos got a whiff of the crocodile's breath. Phew, did his breath *stink*!

"My bird and I just came back from vacation," said the crocodile. "We went to the Amazon jungle."

"Where's that?" asked Amos.

"On the other side of the Atlantic Ocean."

Amos stared at the crocodile. Although he was not sure what, exactly, the Atlantic

Ocean was, he had a feeling it was very far away. "You went all that way for a vacation?" he cried out in amazement.

"Sure, why not?" said the crocodile. He acted like it was no big deal. "That's where Tawaza wanted to go."

"Tawaza?" asked Amos.

"My bird," replied the crocodile. "She's an Egyptian plover. She goes into my mouth and gets the gunk out of my teeth."

Amos was aghast. The crocodile's breath stank to high heavens! Amos could not imagine a bird—or any creature, for that matter—venturing into the crocodile's mouth. He was surprised the bird did not pass out from the smelly fumes.

Just thinking about it made Amos shudder. And yet, as incredible as this was, Amos was about to hear something even more incredible.

Chapter Fourteen
THE CUTEST QUESTIONS

So where are you all going on vacation?" asked the crocodile.

"The Serengeti," said Amos.

"Been there! Done that!" said the crocodile.

"Was it fun?" asked Amos.

"It's a little touristy, but it was okay," said the crocodile. "Tawaza wanted to go. Incidentally, my name is Makizi."

Amos introduced himself. Then he introduced Akka, Cha, Kumba, and Amoeba. Everyone said hello to one another.

"Hey, okay if Tawaza takes a look at that nest on top of your head?" asked the crocodile. "She saw it, and now *she* wants to build a nest on top of *my* head."

Amos could not believe his ears. "You mean, you don't mind if a bird builds a nest on top of your head?" he asked.

"Mind? Why would I mind?" asked the crocodile. "I want my bird to have fun. Tawaza, tell Amos what you call me."

Amos lifted his eyes to the Egyptian plover that was perched on the crocodile's head. "I call him Mr. Fun," she said.

"Mr. Fun?" cried Amos.

The crocodile chuckled. "Isn't she cute? So what do you say? Okay if Tawaza takes a look?"

"It's fine by me," said Amos. "But it's not my nest."

"It's mine!" said Amoeba. "It's okay! You

can come look at my nest! Come look! Come look!"

The Egyptian plover flew over to Amos's head. "So what did you use to build the nest?" asked Tawaza.

"Reeds, grass, mud," replied Kumba, who had built the nest.

"And don't forget ingenuity," said Cha. "It's not any bird that can build a nest on a hippo's slippery bald head."

"She's one awesome bird, my Kumba!" said Akka proudly.

"How long do the reeds need to be?" asked the Egyptian plover.

While the birds discussed nest building, Amos thought he'd ask Makizi more about the Serengeti. "So what kind of animals did you see on the Seren—" he began to ask when the crocodile stopped him.

"Shh—listen!" he whispered. "Don't you just love it?"

"Love what?" asked Amos.

"Tawaza," he said. "Listen to her. Doesn't she ask the cutest questions?"

Amos did not think her questions were so cute. In fact, he was kind of surprised Tawaza had to ask so many questions. She didn't seem to know very much about nest building.

"Well, we should be on our way," said Amos, who was anxious to get going.

Tawaza thanked Amoeba for letting her see her nest. Then she thanked Kumba and Cha for all their advice on building a nest. Then she flew back onto Makizi's head.

"You have a great time at the Serengeti, you hear?" said the crocodile. Then, with a mighty swoosh of his long, reptilian tail, Makizi swung around and swam away.

Amos turned to head down the river again. "That Egyptian plover didn't seem to know very much about nest building," he said.

"Why would she?" sniffed Cha in a haughty voice. "She's an Egyptian plover!"

Amos didn't understand what that had to do with anything. "So?" he said.

"So Egyptian plovers don't build nests," replied Cha. "They bury their eggs in the sandy riverbank."

Chapter Fifteen
MR. FUN

While Amos paddled down the river, he thought about Makizi, the crocodile, and Tawaza, the Egyptian plover. It shocked Amos that the crocodile didn't mind if Tawaza built a nest on top of his head. (And to think she wasn't even the kind of bird that builds a nest!) Amos would never allow such a thing. Oh, sure, he had let Kumba build a nest on his head, but it wasn't as if Kumba had first asked his permission.

"No wonder Tawaza thinks Makizi is

Mr. Fun," thought Amos. "He lets her do whatever she darn well pleases. Well, just wait till we get to the Serengeti," Amos said to himself. "Amoeba will have so much fun, she'll start calling me Mr. Fun, too!"

Amos swam faster. He was eager to get to the Serengeti so they could start having fun.

As Amos floated down the river, he caught a glimpse of his reflection in the water. He certainly did not look like Mr. Fun now. He looked like Mr. Old-Stick-in-the-Mud. There was no smile on his face, no glimmer or sparkle in his eyes.

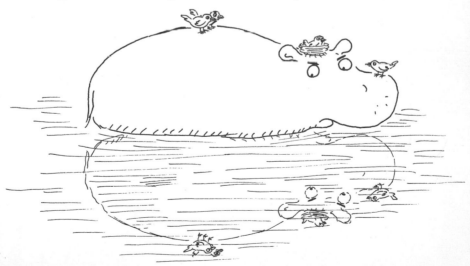

Amos did not want to look like Mr. Old-Stick-in-the-Mud. He wanted to look like Mr. Fun. Amos made up his mind that he was not going to let Akka, Kumba, or Cha spoil his vacation. He was going to start being Mr. Fun—right this very moment!

"This trip sure is fun, isn't it?" he said.

Amos was hoping that Amoeba, who was on top of his head, would respond. But she didn't. But Akka, who was perched at the end of Amos's nose, did.

"Well, well, well!" cried Akka, grinning. "I see you've cheered up, Amos! Didn't I tell you you'd feel lots better once we got under way? You're just like me. I, too, used to get horribly homesick when I left home. I used to travel far and wide looking for a job. I went to Egypt, Kenya, South Africa, the Philippines—you name it! I'm so glad my days of job hunting are over! I love my new job!"

"When we get back home," said Amos, still trying to be cheerful, "I'm going to make a special point of getting to know your new boss better, Akka. He must be a very understanding fellow. Not many hippos would allow their tick bird to go on vacation so soon after starting a brand-new job."

Akka stopped grinning. A look of alarm came across his face. "What are you trying to say, Amos?" he asked.

"What do you mean?" asked Amos.

"You're trying to say something, aren't you?"

"I thought I said it," said Amos.

"No, you didn't," said Akka.

"I didn't?" said Amos.

Akka shook his head. "You're like me,"

he said. "You're too nice of a guy to come right out and say it. But I know what you're trying to say."

"You do?" said Amos. "What?"

"You're trying to say I should not have gone on vacation so soon after I started a brand-new job."

"Am I trying to say that?" said Amos, surprised.

"And you're right, Amos!" wailed Akka. "What am I, nuts? I never should have gone on vacation! Now I've surely lost my job!"

"What's wrong, dear?" asked Kumba from the top of Amos's head.

"You're married to a blithering idiot, honey, that's what's wrong!" moaned Akka. "After years and years of searching for a job, I finally get one and what do I do? I go on vacation! I should have my head examined!"

Kumba flew down to Amos's nose to try to comfort her husband. Amos thought he should try to comfort Akka, too, but he decided to keep his big mouth shut. He had caused enough trouble.

"So much for trying to be Mr. Fun," thought Amos.

Chapter Sixteen
A DISAGREEMENT

Amos made good progress that afternoon. They traveled miles down the river. For the most part, it was very easy traveling. The river was deep and wide, and the current moved right along. While Amos swam, Akka sat on his nose, slouching, looking very dejected.

"I've lost my job!" Akka moaned over and over again, shaking his head. "I just know it!"

"You don't know that for sure," said Amos.

"Yes, I do, Amos!" replied Akka in despair. "I never should have gone on this vacation! Never! What was I thinking?"

"Well, you can always fly back up the river and return to work," suggested Amos.

Akka shook his head. "What's the use?" he said. "The damage is done!"

It wasn't just Akka who was upset. So was Kumba. She was upset that Akka was upset. Kumba did her best to console Akka. But he was inconsolable. Even Cha, in her own way, tried to cheer up Akka. "Oh, don't be such a loser!" she told him. Strangely, though, this only made Akka feel worse.

Amoeba also tried to make her father feel better. She flew down to Amos's nose and gave Akka a big hug and a little piece of reed from her nest.

This made Akka even more misty-eyed. "What a dear child!" he said, wiping his eyes with the tips of his wings.

Amoeba was about to hop back up onto Amos's head when Kumba flew down and landed beside her. She had something in her beak. She set it down in front of Amoeba. It was a bug.

"Amoeba, you didn't eat all of your lunch," said Kumba.

"I don't want any more lunch!" replied Amoeba.

"But it's good for you!" said Kumba. "Now be a good little bird and eat your last bug. You want to grow up to be big and strong like Amos, don't you?"

"No!" said Amoeba.

"Yes, you do!" said Kumba.

"No, I don't!"

"Yes, you do!"

"No, I don't!"

"Yes, you do!"

As the two birds disagreed, the bug began to crawl away. It scurried up Amos's face, between his eyes. Amos, crossing his pupils, watched the bug as it made its way higher and higher up his big face.

"Um, excuse me, Kumba and Amoeba," he said. "I don't mean to interrupt, but the bug seems to have crawled away."

"Hey, let's let Amos decide!" cried Kumba suddenly.

"Let's let Amos decide what?" asked Amos.

"We'll let you decide if Amoeba has to eat her bug," said Kumba.

Chapter Seventeen
AMOS DECIDES

Amos had never had to make a decision like this before. It was a tough decision to make. He had to pick one bird over another. Amoeba and Kumba did not make his life any easier.

"Please say no! Please say no! Please say no!" begged Amoeba.

"Please say yes! Please say yes! Please say yes!" begged Kumba.

Amos did not know *what* to say. He did not want to go against Kumba. But he also did not want Amoeba to think he was an old fuddy-dud who made little tick birds eat every last one of their bugs for lunch. Amos wondered what Makizi, the crocodile, would do in a situation like this. He would be Mr. Fun, that's what!

"No, Amoeba doesn't have to eat the bug if she doesn't want to," said Amos.

"I don't?" cried Amoeba. She looked stunned. Then delighted. Clearly, this was not what Amoeba was expecting to hear.

"Yippee! Amos says I don't have to eat the bug!"

"How about later?" asked Kumba as she peered up into Amos's large eyes.

"What about later?" asked Amos.

"If Amoeba wants to eat the bug later, can she?"

"Sure, I don't see why not," replied Amos.

"How about if she *doesn't* want to eat the bug later?" asked Kumba.

"Well, then, I guess she doesn't have to eat it," replied Amos.

"What if she's not sure?" asked Kumba.

"Not sure?" said Amos.

"Yes, what if she's not sure if she wants to eat the bug later or not?"

"Well, if that's the case," said Amos, "I'm not really sure myself."

"*You're* not sure?" said Kumba.

"Well, no, not if she's not sure."

"But you're sure now, right?" asked Kumba.

"Yes, I'm sure now," replied Amos.

"Are you sure?" asked Kumba.

"Yes, Kumba, I'm sure!" said Amos, growing more and more exasperated with the direction the conversation was taking—which seemed to be nowhere.

"Okay, just as long as you're sure," said Kumba. Lifting her wings, she flew back up onto Amos's head and perched beside Cha.

"I couldn't help listening," Amos heard Cha say to Kumba. "Don't take it personally, Kumba, that Amos has so much trouble understanding things. He's not exactly the sharpest beast in the jungle, if you know what I mean."

Chapter Eighteen
COMPETITION

Amos was glad Kumba was gone. Now he could talk to Amoeba alone. Not that she was really alone. Akka was also on the end of Amos's nose, just a few inches away from where Amoeba was happily hopping about. (Amoeba was still very happy about not having to eat the bug.) But from the glum look on Akka's face, Amos could tell that Akka was in no mood for conversation—particularly the lighthearted banter that Amos had in mind.

"So tell me, Amoeba," said Amos as, smiling, he fixed his gaze only on Amoeba. "What have you been doing all morning on top of my head?"

"Playing with Nungwe."

"Oh? What were you playing?"

"We were having a stawing contest."

"Really?" said Amos. "You know who's an old pro at staring contests?"

"Who?"

"Me!" said Amos.

"Nungwe is an old pwo, too!" said Amoeba.

"I'm an older pro than Nungwe. I once stared at another hippopotamus for three minutes without once blinking."

"Nungwe once stawed at a hippopotamouse for thwee million minutes without once blinking!"

"She did?" said Amos. He was impressed. Then he reminded himself that Nungwe was just a figment of Amoeba's imagination. "Well, I bet Nungwe can't hold her breath as long as I can," said Amos. "I can hold my breath for five minutes."

"Nungwe can hold her bweath for five billion minutes!"

They went from topic to topic, from one glorious accomplishment to another.

Everything Amos could do, Nungwe could do better. Amos found himself in fierce competition with Nungwe. Amos knew Nungwe was not a real bird. But she was real in Amoeba's eyes, and so Amos wanted to be better than Nungwe. As Amos quickly found out, though, this was no easy task. He began to hate the darn little bird.

"It's a good thing she's not real," thought Amos. "Because if she were and she were here now, this vacation would turn real ugly, real fast!"

"I'm going to go play with Nungwe," said Amoeba. "You don't mind, do you, Amos?"

"No, I don't mind," grumbled Amos as Amoeba flew back up to her nest.

For the next hour or so, Amos just floated down the river. He did not say a word. He was racking his brain, trying to think of something he could do better than Nungwe. He was determined to find something—*anything*!

It was hard to think of something, though, with Akka perched on the tip of his nose, looking so gloomy. Amos wished that if Akka was going to sit and mope, he'd go sit and mope on Amos's back, where Amos did not have to look at him all day long.

It was a hot, steamy afternoon. Over on shore, monkeys chattered in the treetops. Cicadas buzzed. Then Amos heard something else.

Off in the distance, thunder, deep and rolling, grumbled. Amos lifted his eyes skyward. Dark, billowy clouds were lurking overhead. It could mean only one thing.

A thunderstorm was approaching!

Chapter Nineteen
THE THUNDERSTORM

Amos turned to head in to shore.

"Why are we going in?" asked Cha.

"A thunderstorm is coming," replied Amos. "Don't want to be out in the river when a thunderstorm hits."

"Nungwe isn't afwaid of thunderstowms," said Amoeba.

"She isn't?" said Amos, surprised. He just assumed every creature in the animal kingdom was afraid of thunderstorms.

"No! Not at all!" replied Amoeba.

"Well, I'm not afraid of thunderstorms, either," said Amos.

And just to prove it, Amos swam back out into the middle of the river. He told the tick birds to stay right where they were. He was worried that they might fly away at the first drop of rain and then there would be no one around to see how brave he was.

A giant raindrop splattered on Amos's nose. It landed just inches from where Akka sat, moping, with his shoulders hunched over. Another fat raindrop fell on Amos. This one splattered on his back. Then there was another loud burst of thunder.

Amos could feel his heart thumping. The truth was, he did not like thunderstorms. Not one bit. He certainly did not like being out in the river during a thunderstorm. He knew it was dangerous and foolhardy. But if Nungwe was not afraid to be in a thunderstorm, well, then, darn it, neither was he!

It began to rain—*hard*! A wild, wet gust of wind blew across the river. The trees on shore heaved this way and that. Huge raindrops pelted the river—as well as Amos and the tick birds.

Still, Amos continued swimming. He was determined to prove that he was braver than Nungwe. There was something else Amos was determined to prove. He wanted to show that, even in a thunderstorm, he was Mr. Fun. He began to sing with great gusto:

"I'm singing in the rain! Just singing in the rain! What a glorious feeling, I'm happy ag—"

Suddenly, just down the river, a gigantic bolt of lightning pierced the black sky. Thunder exploded above his head.

Amos, trembling with fear, had seen—and heard—enough. He stopped singing and whirled about and swam toward shore. Amos sighed. Once again, Nungwe had beaten him. In the Who's Braver in a Thunderstorm contest, the little tick bird who wasn't even real had won.

When he got to shore, Amos took shelter under the jungle's great leafy canopy. He heard the tap-tap-tap-tap of rain on the leaves above him. Then he heard the splat-splat-splat-splat of rain as it dribbled off the leaves and onto him.

Lightning flashed. It lit up the whole jungle!

There was another crack of thunder—the loudest yet.

It startled Amos. It also startled the tick birds. They zipped down and huddled close beside Amos. Amos had never seen tick birds move so fast.

To keep the tick birds dry, Amos lifted his huge hippopotamus head and held it over the birds like an umbrella. Amos was a marvelous umbrella. He kept Akka, Kumba, Cha, and Amoeba perfectly dry. In fact, the tick birds were so dry and comfortable, they fell asleep. But not Amos. He did not get any sleep that night. How could he? He had to keep his head up so the tick birds would not get wet.

"I'd like to see Nungwe keep four birds dry with her puny little head!" thought Amos.

Chapter Twenty
A Real Dilemma

In the morning, Amos had a stiff neck from holding his head in one place for such a long period of time, and shadows under his eyes from lack of sleep. The forest was dripping wet on account of all the rain. But the sun was shining brightly through gaps in the lush green leaves above, and things were already beginning to dry out. Even at this early hour, the jungle was humming with activity. Birds were flitting about. Monkeys were dangling from vines and leaping from branch to branch in the trees.

There was one good thing, Amos discovered, about being on vacation with four tick birds. He did not have to worry about bugs and ticks biting him. For the last few days, the tick birds had been gobbling up every bug and tick in sight. In fact, as it turned out, Amos did not have enough bugs and ticks on his body to feed his passengers. So that morning the tick birds flew off to go look for another big animal whose bugs and ticks they could eat for breakfast. When they returned, Amos set off down the river.

To Amos's delight, Amoeba flew onto his nose to keep him company. Amos was glad to see her. For one thing, it meant he had someone else to look at besides gloomy old Akka. For another, he could try once again to show Amoeba just how much fun he was.

But before Amos could even say a word, Amoeba said, "Guess what?"

"What?" asked Amos.

"Nungwe ate a bug this big at bweakfast!" Amoeba held out her small wings as far apart as she could stretch them. "Isn't Nungwe amazing? She's the most amazing animal I know. She's also vewy smart! Did you know that? She is! She's the smartest animal I know. All the other animals hate Nungwe! That's because she's so smart. Well, not all the animals hate Nungwe. Not me! I don't hate Nungwe! That's because I'm Nungwe's best fwiend!"

For the next hour or so, all Amoeba talked about was Nungwe.

Nungwe! Nungwe! Nungwe!

Amos thought he would scream. Couldn't Amoeba talk about anything else besides Nungwe? Amos was sick and tired of hearing about Nungwe. At last, Amoeba flew back to her nest.

With a sigh, Amos let the current carry him along. He floated down the river all morning. At one point, he came around a bend. Up ahead, he saw something very startling. He stopped swimming and, bewildered, just stared.

The river split in two! Amos did not know which way to go.

Amos treaded water as he tried to figure out what to do. It was a real dilemma. So far as Amos could remember, the vulture hadn't said anything about the river splitting in two.

"What seems to be the problem down there?" demanded Cha from the top of Amos's head. "Why have we stopped?"

"The river splits in two," replied Amos. "I'm not sure which way to go."

"What do you mean you're not sure?" said Cha.

"Nungwe knows which way to go!" said Amoeba, flying from her nest and landing on Amos's nose. "It's this way!" She pointed her wing toward the river that branched off to the right.

This was, in fact, the way Amos was also

thinking of taking. But not now! Not after he heard Nungwe thought this was the way to go.

"That shows how *little* Nungwe knows!" said Amos. He tilted his head toward the river that branched off to the left, and said, "It's *this* way!"

"That's not what Nungwe says," said Amoeba.

"Well, Nungwe is *wrong!*" said Amos.

"I don't think so!" said Amoeba.

"I think so!" said Amos.

"Well, don't blame Nungwe if it's the wong way!" said Amoeba.

"Don't worry!" said Amos. "It's *not* the wrong way!"

Before Amoeba could say another word about Nungwe, Amos swam down the river that branched off to the left.

Chapter Twenty-one
BIG PROBLEMS

For the next several days, Amos ferried the tick birds down the river. He swam very quickly. He was no longer trying to be Mr. Fun. He was just trying to get to the Serengeti as fast as possible so they could start having fun.

With each day that passed, the vacation was steadily going downhill. Nobody seemed to be having a good time. Certainly not Akka. He was miserable about his job. Kumba wasn't having any fun, either. She was worried about Akka. And because Kumba wasn't having a good time, neither was Cha. And now even Amoeba did not seem to be having much fun. That was because of Nungwe. Nungwe was unhappy because it was taking so long to get to the Serengeti.

"Nungwe is bored!" Amoeba flew down every few minutes to tell Amos. "Are we almost at the Soowoongetti yet?"

"Almost," replied Amos each time, and swam even faster.

The truth was, though, that Amos had also begun to wonder the very same thing. When would they get to the Serengeti? It seemed to be taking forever! The vulture had said that the Serengeti was about a three-day trip down the river. Amos and the tick birds had been traveling for more than three days. Indeed, it had been six days since they had left home!

Then, suddenly, it dawned on Amos what must have happened.

"*Oh, no!*" he thought. "I bet I took the wrong turn! Back when the river split in two, we should've gone the other way!"

Amos, fuming, gritted his teeth.

"This is all Nungwe's fault!" he muttered to himself. "If it weren't for that darn little tick bird, I would have gone down the other river! We'd be at the Serengeti now—and having lots and lots of fun!"

Amos sighed. Now he had problems. Big problems! What should he do? He couldn't tell the tick birds that he had taken the wrong river. Well, he could, but if he did, he would be admitting that he had made a mistake. Worse, he would be admitting that Nungwe was right and he was wrong.

There was no way Amos was going to do that!

Amos could think of only one thing to do. Keep quiet! Don't say a thing! Just continue down the river as if nothing were wrong.

So that's what Amos did. He did not say a word. He gave no clue whatsoever that he knew they were heading down the wrong river. While Amos floated along, he kept a sharp eye out for any animal who might be able to give him directions on another way to get to the Serengeti.

One afternoon the tick birds all flew off to look for bugs to eat for lunch. Amos, meanwhile, sat alone on the riverbank and waited for them to return. As he sat there, he saw, just up the shore, a huge gray animal step out from the jungle. Then he spotted two, then three, then four huge gray animals stepping out of the jungle!

Elephants! A whole herd of them! It was a small herd, but it was a whole herd just the same. They had come to the river to get a drink of water. Elephants loved to travel from place to place. Surely they would be able to tell him how to get to the Serengeti!

Chapter Twenty-two
A Close Call

Amos hurried over to where the elephants were gathered on the shore, slurping up water with their trunks. Just as Amos was about to introduce himself to one of the elephants, he froze.

There, on top of the elephant, was Cha!

She was racing about on the elephant's back, gobbling up bugs. Then Amos spotted Kumba, Akka, and Amoeba. All of them were on other elephants, gobbling up bugs.

Evidently, today's lunch was elephant bugs!

Amos ducked behind a bush. His entire body was trembling. Had Cha or any of the other tick birds seen him? Amos glanced from behind his bush. They were still zipping about on the elephants' backs, searching for bugs. They hadn't seen him.

"Whew, that was a close call!" murmured Amos.

Keeping out of sight, Amos slunk from bush to bush until he got to an elephant without a tick bird.

"Psst!" he whispered from his hiding place in the bushes.

The elephant lifted her head and glanced about. She looked puzzled. She could not figure out who was trying to get her attention.

"Over here!" whispered Amos. He lifted his head above the bushes.

The elephant stared at him. Her eyes widened.

"My name is Amos," whispered Amos. "I need your help."

"I'll say you do!" said the elephant.

"Shh!" whispered Amos. "Not so loud! I'm trying to keep a low profile."

"I don't blame you, Mtambo," whispered the elephant.

"*Mtambo?*" said Amos.

"Yes, that's your name, isn't it?"

"No, it's Amos!"

"Amos! Why did I call you Mtambo? I'm so bad with names!"

"As I was saying," whispered Amos, "I need your help."

"Don't worry! I'll take care of everything!" said the elephant. And with that, she lifted the end of her trunk toward Amos's head. The next thing Amos knew, the elephant had started to vacuum up Amoeba's nest!

Amos, horrified, leaped back. "What are you doing?" he cried.

"You said you needed my help," said the elephant.

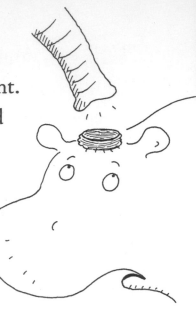

"I don't need *that* kind of help!" said Amos, trying to keep his voice down.

"I thought you wanted me to get rid of that unsightly blemish on top of your head," said the elephant.

"That's not an unsightly blemish!" whispered Amos. "That's a bird's nest. It's supposed to be there!"

"It *is?*" said the elephant, startled. "I thought that was why you were hiding. I thought you were so embarrassed by it, you didn't want anyone to see you."

"No!" said Amos. "That nest belongs to a little tick bird."

"I've never seen a hippopotamus with a bird's nest on top of his head," remarked the elephant. "What does it feel like to have a nest on top of your head? It must feel scratchy. Does it? I'd go crazy if I had a bird's nest on top of my head. I give you a lot of credit, Magugu."

"You mean Amos," said Amos.

"I mean *Amos*!" said the elephant. She gave herself a good whack on top of the head with the end of her trunk. "Where *is* my brain today?"

Amos could see that this elephant was not going to be as helpful as he had hoped. As luck would have it, though, at that moment, Amos spotted an old giraffe on the other side of the river.

Chapter Twenty-three
THE OLD GIRAFFE

Amos thanked the elephant for all her help (even though she really wasn't much help). Then, being very careful that none of the tick birds saw him, Amos slipped into the river and swam over to the opposite shore. The old giraffe stood browsing on some branches that were growing way up high in a tree. Amos scrambled up onto the riverbank. He tilted his head way back so he could get a better view of the old giraffe's face.

"Hello up there!" cried Amos. "My name is Amos and—"

Suddenly, without warning, the old giraffe spit out the leaves he was munching on. Bits of green leaves went flying into the air. They went everywhere—but mostly on Amos.

"Good Lord!" cried the old giraffe. "Did you say I'm eating *moss*?"

"No, I said my name is *Amos*!" said Amos. He shook himself to get rid of the bits of green leaves that were splattered on his face and body.

"You're a *what*?" said the old giraffe.

"I said my name is A-MOS!"

"Who's Amos?" asked the old giraffe.

"I'M AMOS!"

"I'm sorry," said the old giraffe. "I'm a little hard of hearing."

Amos spoke louder. "I need your help."

"What's that you say?" said the old giraffe.

"I need your help!" said Amos again.

"I'm sorry, I don't have any felp," replied the old giraffe. "In fact, I don't even know what felp is."

"Not felp, *help*!" said Amos. "I said I need your *help*!"

The old giraffe, Amos noticed, was eyeing him in the most curious sort of way.

"I see you're looking at the nest that's on my head," said Amos.

"What did you say?" asked the old giraffe.

"I said I see you're looking at the nest on my head."

"You've got *what* in your bed?"

"Not bed—HEAD!" shouted Amos.

"I thought you said you had a pest in your bed," said the old giraffe.

"No, I said I see you're looking at the NEST on my HEAD!"

"Yes, I see it," said the old giraffe, gazing down at Amos. "I didn't want to say anything because I didn't know if you knew about it."

"Yes, I know all about it," said Amos. "It belongs to a little tick bird."

"It belongs to a little sick bird?"

"No, a little *tick* bird!" said Amos.

"I can't hear a word you're saying," said the old giraffe. "Speak up!" He said it in a very grumpy voice. Amos got the feeling that the old giraffe thought it was Amos's fault he couldn't be heard.

Amos decided to get right to the point. "Do you know how to get to the Serengeti?"

"What's that you say?" said the old giraffe.

"I SAID DO YOU KNOW HOW TO GET TO THE SERENGETI?" cried Amos at the top of his lungs.

And then one of the worst things that could possibly happen at that moment happened. Amos heard a fluttering sound behind him. He turned to take a look.

And there was Amoeba.

Chapter Twenty-four
A Fun Game!

Oh, no!" groaned Amos.

How much had Amoeba heard? Did she hear him ask for directions? Did she know he was lost? Maybe Amoeba had not heard that much. Maybe, just maybe, Amos hoped, she had arrived only seconds ago and had not heard anything.

With a perfectly innocent smile, Amos said, "Amoeba! What a nice surprise! You're probably wondering what I'm doing talking to this old giraffe. Well, I was just trying to find out if he knew of something fun we could do."

Just then, behind him, Amos felt someone hovering over his shoulder. It was the old giraffe. Head lowered, the old giraffe was peering at Amoeba with keen interest.

"Is this the little sick bird you were telling me about?" he asked.

"I'm sick?" cried Amoeba, with big startled eyes.

"Yes, you're a little sick bird," said the old giraffe.

"This kind hippo is taking good care of you."

"I didn't know I was sick!" said Amoeba.

"You're not sick!" said Amos.

"That's not what you told me!" said the old giraffe. "You told me she was a little sick bird!"

"I said a little tick bird!" cried Amos. "T-I-C-K! A LITTLE TICK BIRD!"

"All right already!" said the old giraffe. He sounded very offended. He looked very angry. He glared at Amos and cried, "Gee whiz! You don't have to be a hothead about it! I'm a little hard of hearing, okay? You could show a little more understanding!"

Amos tried to apologize, but the old giraffe spun about and took off in a huff.

"So what did he say?" asked Amoeba.

"What did who say?" asked Amos.

"That old giwaffe," said Amoeba. "What did he say would be fun for us to do?"

"Oh, well, he didn't really—" Amos began to say when Amoeba interrupted.

"Wait, let me guess! SHOUTING!" she shouted. "HE SAID SHOUTING WOULD BE FUN, DIDN'T HE? HE'S WIGHT! THIS IS FUN! I'M GOING TO GO TELL NUNGWE! SHE'LL LOVE THIS GAME! HEY, NUNGWE, WANT TO PLAY A WEALLY FUN GAME?" cried Amoeba at the top of her lungs, and she flew off.

Chapter Twenty-five
TONGUE-TIED

Alone, Amos flopped down on the riverbank. As he sat there, mulling things over, he noticed a female hippopotamus just a little ways up the river. She was swimming all by herself with her back turned to Amos.

"Hey, a hippo!" thought Amos. "I bet she'll be able to help me!"

Amos plunged into the water. "Excuse me," he said as he swam toward the female hippopotamus. "I wonder if you could help me. I'm trying to get to the Seren—"

Amos stopped in midsentence. That was because the female hippopotamus had turned around. Amos gasped. She was the most gorgeous hippopotamus he had ever seen! She had dazzling brown eyes, the cutest nose, and a soft ruddy-gray complexion.

"Yes?" asked the hippopotamus, smiling sweetly.

"Wow, what a smile!" thought Amos. Flustered, he glanced away. His heart began to pound furiously. He became very shy all of a sudden. And very nervous.

"I, uh, well, er, I, um, gee—" Amos stammered. He was all tongue-tied at being so close to such an astonishingly beautiful creature.

"HEY, GUESS WHO'S BACK?" a little bird's voice shouted in the air just above Amos's head. "ME!"

Amoeba landed softly on Amos's nose.

"Who are you?" asked the hippopotamus, still smiling, her eyes glistening with curiosity.

"I'M AMOEBA!" shouted Amoeba.

"She's, she's, my, um, my, um, that is, my, um—" Amos tried to say.

"Oh, is this another game?" cried Amoeba excitedly, looking at Amos and hopping up and down. "I want to play, too! I, um, er, uh, uh, well, er, um—"

"Oh, so this is a game, is it?" asked the gorgeous hippopotamus, unamused, peering only at Amos. She was no longer smiling. "You're making me your unwitting dupe, aren't you? You just want to make a fool out of me, don't you?"

"Uh, um, er—NO!" cried Amos.

"Uh, um, er—YES!" cried Amoeba.

"You've got some nerve, mister!" said the gorgeous hippopotamus, now glaring at Amos. She whirled about in the water and, fuming, swam off up the river.

"Uh—uh—WAIT!" cried Amos forlornly.

"I don't like this game!" said Amoeba. Then she began to shout: "I LIKE THE SHOUTING GAME BETTER! SO DOES NUNGWE! LET'S PLAY THAT GAME INSTEAD! OKAY, AMOS?"

Amos just groaned.

Chapter Twenty-six
BEDTIME

When the other tick birds returned from lunch, Amos continued down the river. His heart ached. He could not stop thinking about the gorgeous hippopotamus and how he had been unable to talk to her. He hated himself for being so shy and nervous and tongue-tied.

That night Amos and the tick birds camped out among the tall reeds on the riverbank. As dusk was settling over the river and in the jungle, the tick birds gathered on the tip of Amos's nose to watch the fireflies flicker on and off in the gathering darkness. By and by, Kumba put her wing around Amoeba and said, "Bedtime, Amoeba."

Amoeba slipped out from under Kumba's wing. "It's too oily for bedtime!" she said.

"No, it isn't," said Kumba.

"Yes, it is!" said Amoeba.

"No, it isn't!"

"Yes, it is!"

"No!"

"Yes!"

"No!"

"Yes!"

"Let's ask Amos!" said Amoeba, looking over at Amos. "Amos, isn't it too oily for bedtime?"

Amos did not want Amoeba to think he

was an old fussbudget like her mother. So he said, "Yes, it's too early."

"See, I told you it was too oily!" Amoeba told her mother.

"It is too early?" asked Kumba, peering at Amos.

"Yes, it is," replied Amos.

"How early is it?" asked Kumba.

The truth was, Amos did not know. "How early do you think it is, Kumba?" he asked. He thought he was being very clever, turning the question around so Kumba had to answer it.

"Don't you know?" asked Kumba.

"Yes, I know," said Amos.

"Then why do you want to know?" asked Kumba.

"Because I want to see if *you* know, Kumba," said Amos.

"But you do know?"

"Oh, yes, I know," replied Amos.

"Then how early is it?" asked Kumba.

"But if I tell you, Kumba, then I won't know if *you* know."

"But you do know how early it is?" asked Kumba.

"Yes, Kumba, I know!" cried Amos.

For the next ten minutes, Amos and Kumba went back and forth talking like this. In all likelihood, they probably would have continued going back and forth talking like this all night long if it had not been for Amoeba. The little bird finally settled the matter by blurting out, "Good night! I'm going to bed!"

It was not a minute too soon for Amos. He was ready to go to bed himself, he was so exhausted from talking to Kumba.

Chapter Twenty-seven
A CONFESSION

The next morning they were off again, bright and early, down the river. The farther Amos floated down the river, the farther, he realized, he and the tick birds were getting from their true destination, the Serengeti. (And the farther away they were from having lots and lots of fun.) Worse, before long, their vacation would be over. Soon they would have to head back home—without ever seeing the Serengeti or having lots of fun! Amos knew Amoeba and the other tick birds would not be very happy about that.

As much as Amos hated to admit it, he knew he had to say something. He knew he could not continue floating down the river as if everything were perfectly fine when everything was not perfectly fine.

Amos decided he would tell the tick birds that morning about his mistake. But he didn't. He couldn't. He was too nervous. It took him almost until the end of the afternoon to get up the courage to say something.

"Akka, I have a few words I'd like to address to the group," said Amos as they floated down the river. "Would you kindly move up to the top of my head?"

"That's okay, Amos, you don't have to include me in the fun and games," said Akka. "I'm not much in the mood for that sort of thing right now."

"I don't think you have to worry about fun

and games," said Amos. "I have something important to say. So could you please join the others on top of my head?"

"Do I have to, Amos?" asked Akka.

"Yes, you have to," said Amos.

"All right—if you say so," sighed Akka. He flew to the top of Amos's head.

Amos gazed at his reflection in the river. The four birds were perched on top of his head, gazing quizzically down at his reflection in the water.

With his heart thumping wildly, Amos took a deep breath and said, "I have a confession to make . . ."

Chapter Twenty-eight
NOT AMOS'S
FINEST MOMENT

A confession?" Amos heard Cha mutter under her breath. "What kind of a vacation is this?"

Amos continued, "I'm afraid I have some rather bad news to report."

"Bad news?" said Cha. She was no longer muttering under her breath. "What do you mean you have bad news?"

"It concerns our vacation," said Amos. "Do you remember a few days ago when the river split in two?"

"I wemember!" cried Amoeba. "Nungwe

wanted to go one way and you wanted to go the other!"

"Yes, that's right, Amoeba," replied Amos. He was so ashamed of what he was about to say, he could not look the little bird in the eye. (That is, he could not look at the reflection of her little eyes.) "Well, Amoeba, it turns out Nungwe was right."

"She was?" cried Amoeba. She looked very surprised.

"Yes, she was," said Amos. "We should have gone Nungwe's way."

"What are you talking about?" demanded Cha.

"Nungwe's way was the right way to go to the Serengeti," said Amos, his voice quivering.

"You mean this isn't the way to get to the Serengeti?" asked Kumba.

Amos shook his head. "I'm—I'm afraid not, Kumba," he stammered.

"You mean all this time you've been taking us down the wrong river?" said Cha.

"Yes, Cha," replied Amos.

"So we're not going to see the Serengeti?" asked Kumba. She certainly didn't seem to be having any trouble understanding Amos now.

"No," said Amos. He felt terrible. He lowered his head and gazed away from his reflection.

"Oh, I wanted this to be a fun vacation!" he said. "Honestly, I did! But nobody is having fun! Nobody! Akka is unhappy because of something I was trying to say that I wasn't trying to say. Kumba is unhappy because Akka is unhappy. Cha is unhappy because Kumba is unhappy. Amoeba is unhappy because Nungwe is unhappy. And Nungwe is unhappy because this trip is taking so long. And I'm unhappy because we're not at the Serengeti yet having lots and lots of fun!"

A big tear slid down Amos's chubby gray face. It was not Amos's finest moment. Not by a long shot. Blubbering in front of tick birds was not a very hippo-esque thing to do. But Amos could not help it.

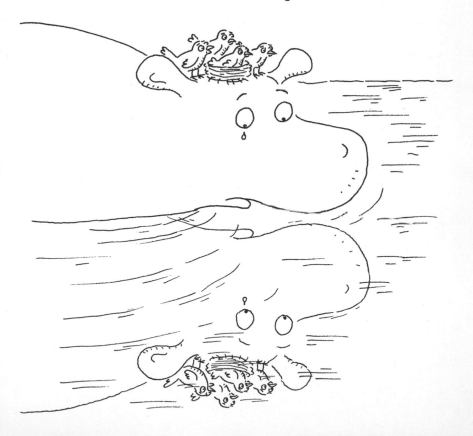

Fighting back tears, Amos lifted his head and gazed at his reflection in the water to see how the tick birds were taking things.

Not well! They all looked shocked. Cha opened her beak to speak, but no words came out.

"Look!" thought Amos. "Everyone is shocked that I've ruined their vacations! Cha can't even find the words to yell at me!"

Chapter Twenty-nine
A STRANGE SOUND

I'm sorry I've ruined everyone's vacation," said Amos.

He waited for Akka, Kumba, Cha, and Amoeba to respond, but none of them spoke. Amos could feel the birds trembling on top of his head.

"They're so mad at me, they're trembling with anger!" thought Amos.

"I don't blame you for being mad at me," he said. "After what I've done, I deserve it!"

Amos paused, hoping the tick birds might find it in their hearts to forgive him.

But they still did not say a thing. They just kept trembling.

"Well . . . ," said Amos, his voice choking up. "I guess we might as well head home."

Then, suddenly, Amos realized something. He was moving fast—very, very fast—down the river!

Amos had been so busy apologizing to the tick birds, he had not been paying attention to the current. Amos heard a strange sound—a loud, thunderous roar. Amos had never heard such a sound. Whatever it was, the river was quickly pulling him toward it.

The tick birds were not trembling with anger, Amos now realized. They were trembling with fear. They were frightened at this thunderous roar that they—and Amos—were all heading toward. They were so afraid, they were paralyzed. They couldn't even fly off!

Amos, gasping, swung around and began to swim upstream, away from the thunderous roar. No luck! The current was too strong. It swept Amos swiftly downstream like a leaf.

The roar got louder and louder. Amos, petrified, closed his eyes.

The next thing Amos knew, he was flying, like a bird, through the wet, misty air.

Chapter Thirty
RAPIDS!

WWWWhhhhOOOoooaaahhhhHHH!"
cried Amos as he fell with a *plop!* into a pool
of swirling, foaming white water.

Amos opened his eyes. He had gone
over a waterfall. Luckily, it was just a small
waterfall.

The river was still flowing very, very fast.
It was also white and foamy and splashing
furiously up against enormous smooth rocks.
Amos, panicking, struggled to swim to shore.
He swam with all his might, but he got no-
where. He just swam in place. Amos had

never been in a situation like this before. Never! The force of the current was too strong for Amos. It swept him over a ledge. Off Amos went down the rushing white river.

"Rapids!" shouted Akka. "Hold on, everyone!"

Amos felt four pairs of bird claws dig into the top of his skull. The tick birds held on to him for dear life. Unfortunately for Amos, he had no one he could hold on to for dear life. All he could do was shoot down the rapids, hold his head high above the water so the tick birds would be safe, and hope for the best.

"Oomph!" he cried as he smacked into a big, smooth, slippery rock that was sticking up out of the water.

"Umph!" cried Amos as he slammed into another slippery rock. *"Oomph-oomph-*

oomph!" he blurted out as he hit a series of smaller rocks.

Amos went barreling over a ledge of cascading water. He found himself spinning about in a whirlpool. Round and round he went! Then off he went, rocketing down more rapids—and smacking into more rocks.

Bump! Bump! Bump!

"Oomph! Ooomph! Ooomph!"

As Amos splashed and swirled about in the rapids, he did his best to keep his head above the water. He did not want Amoeba or any of the other tick birds to be swept overboard or get hurt.

Amos hurled down the fast, furious, swirling, foaming river.

Would these rapids *ever* stop?

And then, just when Amos was sure he would never see a lazy-flowing river again, the rapids ceased. The river widened and returned to its gentle, peaceful, quiet flow.

Chapter Thirty-one
A Brilliant Plan

Amos heaved a huge sigh of relief. "Thank goodness that's over!" he thought.

"Is everyone okay?" he asked.

There was no response from the top of his head.

"Oh, no!" thought Amos. Amoeba and the other tick birds hadn't been swept overboard, had they?

Amos was too afraid to look at his reflection. He was too worried at what he might find—nothing! Just a big, bald, vacant head. Holding his breath, Amos glanced down at the water.

Everyone was okay! Amoeba, Akka, Kumba, and Cha were still on top of his head. They were huddled in Amoeba's nest. They were sopping wet. They seemed to be in a daze.

Amoeba was the first to snap out of her trance.

"Wheeeeeeee!" she cried. "That was fun!"

"Lots of fun!" said Kumba.

"Lots and lots of fun!" said Cha.

"That was brilliant, Amos!" said Akka.

Amos could scarcely believe his ears. "You—you mean you're not mad?"

"Us? *Mad?*" said Kumba. She sounded surprised.

"Why on earth would we be mad?" asked Cha.

"Come on, Amos!" said Akka. "You can stop with the shenanigans! We're on to you!"

"You are?" said Amos. He had no idea what Akka was talking about.

"Yes, we are!" said Akka, chuckling. "You had no intention of going to the Serengeti. That was just a ruse! You just said it so you could surprise us by taking us down those rapids. Well, it worked, Amos!"

"It sure did!" said Kumba.

"I'll say!" cried Cha, shaking herself dry.

Amos tried to explain that he had no intention of going down the rapids. Really he hadn't! But the tick birds did not believe him.

"You probably had this whole thing planned right from the start of the trip, didn't you?" said Akka. "To think we actually believed you when you said we were going to the Serengeti."

"But we *were*!" insisted Amos.

"There he goes again!" said Akka.

Amos could not help but notice the change in Akka's mood. He was absolutely radiant.

"I see you're back to your old cheerful self, Akka," said Amos.

"You bet I am!" said Akka, with a big grin. "And I have *you* to thank for it, Amos! Those rapids were just the thing I needed to snap me out of my doldrums. You knew I needed a good jolt. It was a brilliant plan, Amos! Absolutely brilliant!"

"But what about your job?" Amos asked. The moment he said it, Amos wished he hadn't. He was worried that it would make Akka glum again.

But it didn't! Akka grinned and said, "Job schmob! Amos, my friend, there are more important things in life than just work. Don't get me wrong! I certainly hope I still have my job when I get back home. But you know what?"

"What?" asked Amos.

"If I've lost it, I've lost it. There'll be other jobs," said Akka. "But there may not be other times we'll all be together like this, having fun. You know what I'm trying to say, don't you, Amos?"

Amos was worried he might say the wrong thing again. He did not want Akka to think he was trying to say something that he was not trying to say. So he replied, "Mmm." He hoped "Mmm" was a safe thing to say.

"Of course you know what I'm trying to say!" cried Akka with a hearty chuckle. "You and I are just alike, Amos! There's no denying it!"

Chapter Thirty-two
AGAIN!

Amos swam to shore and stepped onto the riverbank. Sticking close to the river, he made his way through the thick jungle back up past the rapids. Once he got to where the river wasn't flowing so fast, Amos stepped out onto a sandbar. The narrow spit of land was covered with reeds. He was about to step into the river to swim back home when Amoeba flew down in front of him. She began hopping excitedly up and down on the sand.

"Again!" she cried. "Again!"

"*Again?*" said Amos, puzzled.

"Yes, again! Do it again!"

"Do what again?" asked Amos.

"Go down the wapids again!"

Akka, Kumba, and Cha flew down and landed beside Amoeba.

"What an excellent idea!" cried Akka.

"Please take us down the rapids again, Amos!" said Cha, with her wings clasped together. "Please! Please! Please!"

Amos thought he was hearing and seeing things. Was this really Cha?

"Again!" cried Amoeba as she hopped up and down on the sand. "Again!"

"Well, if you really want to, I guess we can go down the rapids again," said Amos.

"Yippeee!" cried Amoeba. "We're going down the wapids again!"

"Oh, no, you're not!" said Kumba.

"What do you mean oh, no, I'm not?" said Amoeba. "Oh, yes, I am!"

"Oh, no, you're not!" said Kumba. "Those rapids are too dangerous for a little tick bird. You and I will stay here."

"They're not too dangerous!" protested Amoeba.

"They are so too dangerous!" said Kumba. "You're not going down them again!"

"Yes, I am!" said Amoeba.

"No, you're not!" said Kumba.

"Yes, I am!"

"No!"

"Yes!"

"No!"

"Yes!"

"No!"

"Let's ask Amos!" said Amoeba. She flew up to the tip of a reed and stared into Amos's face. "Can I go down the wapids again, Amos?" she asked.

Chapter Thirty-three
AMOS'S BIG CHANCE

Here was Amos's big chance. He could prove to Amoeba, once and for all, that he really was Mr. Fun. All he had to do was let her go down the rapids again.

All he had to do was say one word: "Yes."

"No," said Amos.

Amoeba turned to Kumba with a triumphant look on her face. "There, see!" she said. "Amos says no! *NO?*" She spun about to face Amos. "What do you mean *no?*"

"Kumba is right, Amoeba. Those rapids are too dangerous for a little tick bird."

Amoeba glared at Amos. She looked very angry. "You said we were going to have fun!" she cried. "But you're no fun! You're no fun at all!"

Bursting into tears, Amoeba flew off down the riverbank.

Amos, watching, sighed.

"Oh, dear!" said Kumba. "The rest of you go down the rapids. I'll stay here with Amoeba."

"No, I'll stay," said Amos.

"What are you talking about, Amos?" cried Cha. She was back to her old glowering self. "You can't stay! You have to go down the rapids with us! We need you to sit on!"

Amos spotted a log floating down the river. "Look, there's a log floating down the river," he said. "You can ride down the rapids on it."

"Hey, a log might be fun!" cried Akka.

"Let's do it!" said Cha.

Akka and Cha flew out to the log. But not Kumba. She lingered to talk with Amos.

"You're sure you don't mind staying here with Amoeba?" she asked.

"I'm sure," said Amos. He could tell Kumba really wanted to go down the rapids again.

"You're sure you're sure?"

"Yes, Kumba, I'm sure I'm sure," said Amos.

"You're sure you're sure you're sure?" said Kumba.

"Yes, Kumba, I'm sure I'm sure I'm sure! Now go!" he told her.

Kumba flew off and joined Akka and Cha

on the log. The log floated closer and closer toward the waterfall. The tick birds braced themselves for the plunge.

Suddenly, in the thrill of the moment, Cha shrieked out, "This has been the best vacation ever!"

"That's for sure!" cried Kumba.

"Hold on tight, ladies!" shouted Akka. Then, as the log sailed over the edge of the waterfall, he yelled,

"Yeeeeeeeeee-ha!"

Chapter Thirty-four
A Terrible Catastrophe

Amos walked up the riverbank to look for Amoeba. He found her standing on the sand, sulking, with her wings crossed, staring out at the river. When Amoeba heard Amos coming, she turned her back on him.

"Look, Amoeba, I'm sorry," said Amos. "But Kumba—your mom—is right. Those rapids are too dangerous for a little tick bird."

Amoeba did not say anything. She just made a disgusted grunt and crossed her wings even more tightly.

"Tell you what," said Amos. "When you get a little bigger, you and I will come back here and go down the rapids again."

He waited for a response, but Amoeba did not respond.

"So what do you say?" asked Amos.

But Amoeba still did not respond.

Amos sighed. He was so discouraged. Just when Amoeba was starting to have fun, what happens? Amoeba stops having fun. All because of him. Amos plopped down onto the sand.

Amoeba, gasping, swung around, with her beak wide open. She stared at Amos. She looked shocked.

"What's the matter?" asked Amos.

"You—you—you—" But Amoeba could not get the words out.

"I what?" asked Amos.

"You—you sat down on Nungwe!" cried Amoeba.

"I did *what*?" cried Amos, horrified, leaping to his feet. "Oh, no!"

"Poor Nungwe!" said Amoeba.

Amos stared at the patch of sand where he had been sitting. What a terrible catastrophe! Amoeba would never forgive him now. Amos knew he should apologize, but he did not know who he should apologize to. Amoeba or Nungwe?

"I'm so sorry, Amoeba!" he said. "I didn't

mean to sit down on your friend! What a big klutz I am!"

"It's okay, Amos!" said Amoeba. "Nungwe is fine! She's just a little shaken up! That's all! Look, there she goes! She just flew off! I think she's going to fly home! I don't think Nungwe wants to go home with you! I don't think she twusts you!"

"I don't blame Nungwe!" said Amos. "I wouldn't trust anyone, either, who sat down on me!"

"Thank goodness Nungwe wasn't hurt!" said Amoeba. "I told you she's an amazing bird. Even a big hippopotamouse like you can sit down on her and she doesn't get hurt!"

For once, Amos had to admit that Nungwe truly was an amazing bird.

Chapter Thirty-five
HIDE!

Amoeba peered up at Amos. "Did you weally mean it?" she asked.

"Did I really mean what?" asked Amos.

"Did you weally mean what you said? About us coming back here when I'm a little bigger so we can go down the wapids again?"

"Yes, I really mean it," said Amos. "As soon as you're a little bigger, we'll come back here. We'll go down the rapids again and again and again—as much as you like!"

"Weally?" said Amoeba.

"Really!" said Amos.

Amoeba flew up to a reed to be closer to Amos. "I know this sounds stwange," she said, "but you know what?"

"What?" asked Amos.

"I'm glad Nungwe flew off."

"You are?" said Amos, startled. It did sound strange!

Amoeba nodded. "Yes, but don't tell Nungwe!"

"Don't worry, I won't," promised Amos. Then he asked, "Why are you glad she flew off?"

"Because now you and I can have fun together!" replied Amoeba. "So what do you want to do?"

Amos tried to think of something fun they could do. But the only thing he could think of was to go on a vacation to the Serengeti.

"I know what we can do!" said Amoeba. "We can hide from the others!"

"*Hide?*" said Amos, glancing about. "Hide where?" There was no place to hide. They were on a sandbar surrounded by reeds.

But Amoeba had already darted into the reeds. She waved Amos over with her wing. "Hurry, Amos!" she said. "Before they come back!"

"But Amoeba—"

"*Hide!*" ordered Amoeba.

Amos did as he was told. He followed Amoeba into the reeds and plopped down. Amos was so enormous, he was positive the tick birds would spot him the moment they returned.

"They'll never find us!" whispered Amoeba. She began to giggle. She could not stop. Hearing her, Amos began to giggle. He

could not stop. The two of them giggled and
giggled.

Suddenly, Amos stopped worrying about
trying to find something fun he and Amoeba
could do together. He and Amoeba did not
have to go on a vacation or go down the
rapids or go to the Serengeti—or any other
place—to have fun.

They were doing it right now!

When Akka, Kumba, and Cha flew

back, they had no trouble finding Amos and Amoeba. No trouble whatsoever. But it was not Amos's huge hippopotamus size that gave them away.

It was all the giggling that was coming from within the reeds.